Symbols of American Freedom

The Star-Spangled Banner

by Kirsten Chang

Blastoff! Readers 1

Bellwether Media • Minneapolis, MN

Note to Librarians, Teachers, and Parents:

Blastoff! Readers are carefully developed by literacy experts and combine standards-based content with developmentally appropriate text.

Level 1 provides the most support through repetition of high-frequency words, light text, predictable sentence patterns, and strong visual support.

Level 2 offers early readers a bit more challenge through varied simple sentences, increased text load, and less repetition of high-frequency words.

Level 3 advances early-fluent readers toward fluency through increased text and concept load, less reliance on visuals, longer sentences, and more literary language.

Level 4 builds reading stamina by providing more text per page, increased use of punctuation, greater variation in sentence patterns, and increasingly challenging vocabulary.

Level 5 encourages children to move from "learning to read" to "reading to learn" by providing even more text, varied writing styles, and less familiar topics.

Whichever book is right for your reader, Blastoff! Readers are the perfect books to build confidence and encourage a love of reading that will last a lifetime!

This edition first published in 2019 by Bellwether Media, Inc.

Library of Congress Cataloging-in-Publication Data

LC record for The Star-Spangled Banner available at https://lccn.loc.gov/2017061635

Editor: Rebecca Sabelko Designer: Andrea Schneider

Printed in the United States of America, North Mankato, MN.

Table of Contents

What Is the Star-Spangled Banner?

The Star-Spangled Banner is America's **anthem**.

The song tells a story of strength and **freedom**.

Fly the Flag

In the War of 1812, the British **attacked** the United States.

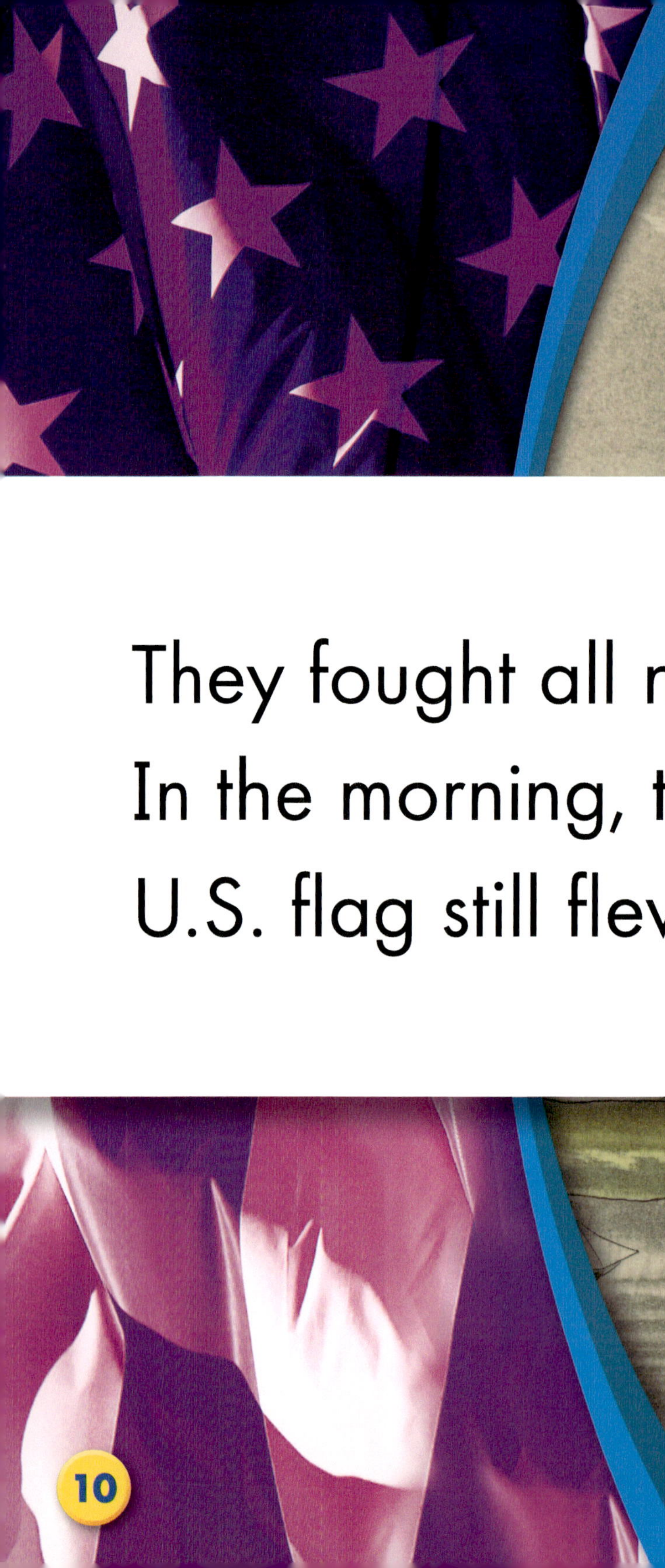

They fought all night.
In the morning, the
U.S. flag still flew.

Battle at
Fort McHenry

Francis Scott Key saw the battle. He wrote a **poem** about the **victory**.

The poem was made into a song. Later, it became the anthem.

Battle of Baltimore

Land of the Free

Today, the song plays at special events. People sing along with the music.

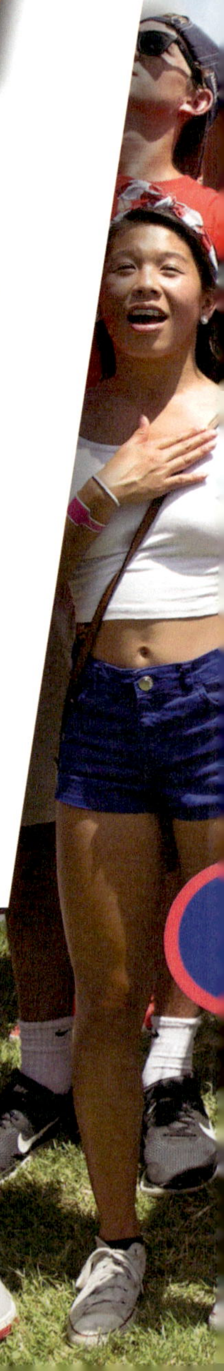

They stand
and place their
right hands over
their hearts.

The song says
the U.S. is the
land of the free!

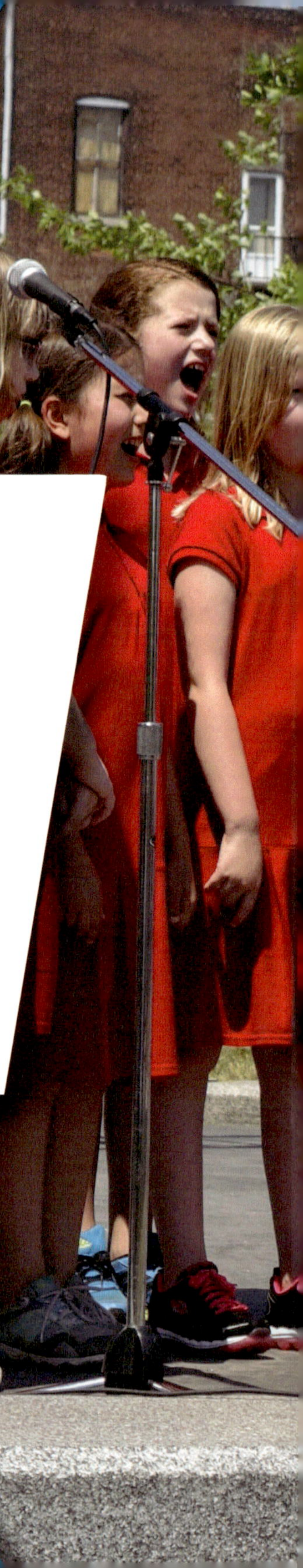

Glossary

anthem

a song of praise

poem

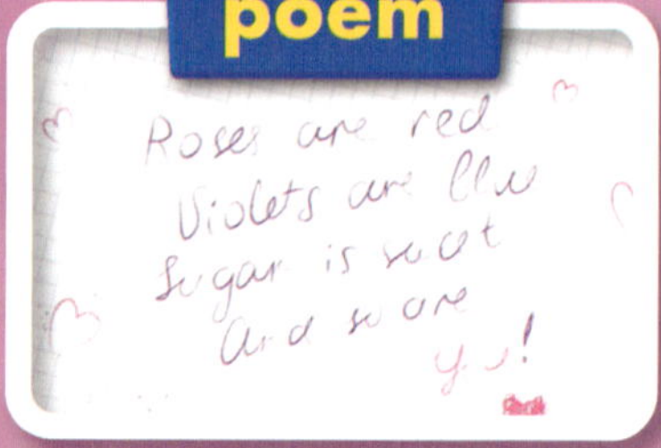

a piece of writing in short lines using words that often rhyme

attacked

used weapons against an enemy in a war

victory

a win in a game or war

freedom

the state of being free

To Learn More

AT THE LIBRARY

Brannon, Cecelia H. *Zoom in on the National Anthem*. New York, N.Y.: Enslow Publishing, 2017.

Chang, Kirsten. *The United States Flag*. Minneapolis, Minn.: Bellwether Media, 2019.

Nelson, Maria. *The National Anthem*. New York, N.Y.: Gareth Stevens Publishing, 2015.

ON THE WEB

Learning more about the Star-Spangled Banner is as easy as 1, 2, 3.

1. Go to www.factsurfer.com.
2. Enter "Star-Spangled Banner" into the search box.
3. Click the "Surf" button and you will see a list of related web sites.

With factsurfer.com, finding more information is just a click away.

Index

The images in this book are reproduced through the courtesy of: Kozlik, front cover; Mormegil/ Wiki Commons, p. 3; DOD Photo/ Alamy, pp. 4-5; 501 collection/ Alamy, pp. 6-7; Kurz & Allison/ Library of Congress, pp. 8-9; John Bower/ Library of Congress, pp. 10-11; Everett Historical, pp. 12-13; Jon Bilous, pp. 14-15; Suzanne Cordeiro/ Getty, pp. 16-17; Cal Sport Media/ Alamy, pp. 18-19; Perry van Munster/ Alamy, pp. 20-21; Aspen Photo, p. 22 (top left); sirtravelalot, p. 22 (middle right); lanitta, p. 22 (top right); Joseph Sohm, p. 22 (middle left); fstop123, p. 22 (bottom left).